Aunt Victoria's Monster

Written by Sally Odgers
Illustrated by Helen Bacon

Contents

Chapter One
Aunt Victoria Tells Me about a Yeti   5

Chapter Two
I Learn about Monster Valley   9

Chapter Three
Mimi Maxwell Asks for Proof   16

Chapter Four
Sperrington Smithers Arrives   25

Chapter Five
Aunt Victoria and I Depart   32

Chapter Six
I See a Part of the Paintbrush Monster   40

Chapter Seven
We Catch a Monster   46

Chapter Eight
The Paintbrush Monster Hitches a Ride   54

Chapter Nine
Aunt Victoria Sets Up a Fund   63

Chapter Ten
Aunt Victoria Moves to a New Location   75

Chapter One

Aunt Victoria Tells Me about a Yeti

Have you ever seen a monster? I have. Just ask Aunt Victoria! She knows, because she saw it, too. But now I'm getting ahead of my story, which all started with Aunt Victoria.

Aunt Victoria has three major interests. The first one is adventuring. She's been to so many places that I can't remember all the names. In every single one, she's had an adventure.

"I just can't seem to help it, Toby," Aunt Victoria once explained. "I don't look for adventures, but adventures always seem to find me anyway." Her voice was plaintive, but her eyes gleamed as she spoke. Somehow, I didn't think she minded having adventures.

Aunt Victoria's second major interest is painting pictures. She paints very quickly and very furiously and she always uses lots and lots of color.

Aunt Victoria's third major interest is monsters. That's right, m-o-n-s-t-e-r-s.

"Monsters aren't real," I scoffed when she mentioned them. "They're made up by people."

"That's what I used to think, too, but I stopped thinking that when the Loch Ness Monster ate my camera," said Aunt Victoria.

I laughed aloud when she said that.

"Don't be silly, Aunt Victoria!" I gasped as soon as I could catch my breath. "Everyone knows the Loch Ness Monster is imaginary."

"Is that so?" asked Aunt Victoria.

"Everyone knows that," I told her, and I laughed again. Imagine having a grown-up aunt who believes in monsters!

Aunt Victoria pointed her paintbrush at my head. "Things that everyone knows often aren't true, Toby," she said. "Did you know that, once upon a time, everyone knew fresh fruit was bad for children? Did you know that, once upon a time, everyone knew that getting a suntan was healthy? I'm telling you, Toby, I don't care what everyone knows. I know what *I* know, and I know what ate my camera."

"All right, Aunt Victoria," I spluttered. "I believe you. If you say you saw the Loch Ness Monster, I'll take your word for it. Tell me about the other monsters you've met."

Aunt Victoria gave me a suspicious look. "No laughing," she said. "I mean that. If I tell you about the monsters I've met, I don't want to catch you laughing behind my back."

"I won't," I promised.

"I saw a yeti once," began Aunt Victoria. "A yeti is a snow monster that lives up in the Himalayas."

"What did it look like?" I asked.

"Well, it was taller than I am, and it was covered with short white hair, like a polar bear," said Aunt Victoria. "It had black, beady eyes, enormous flat feet, and it was eating a banana."

"You don't find bananas in the Himalayas," I said. "Bananas grow in hot places."

"It was eating *my* banana," said Aunt Victoria firmly. "The yeti reached over my shoulder and stole my banana, then it sat down and ate it. After that, it wanted another banana, but I didn't have any, so I gave it a cucumber instead."

"What did it do with the cucumber?" I asked.

"It threw it at me and ran away," she said.

"Have you seen any other monsters?"

"I saw a sea serpent in the Bahamas once, and I saw a tulip monster in Rotterdam. The most interesting monster I ever saw, though, was the Paintbrush Monster of Monster Valley," said Aunt Victoria.

"Where's Monster Valley?" I asked.

Aunt Victoria shook her head. "I can't tell you," she said, helping herself to one of my favorite peppermints. "Monster Valley isn't on the map."

Chapter Two

I Learn about Monster Valley

That seemed really weird to me.

"How did you get to Monster Valley if it isn't on the map?" I asked. "How did you know it was there?"

"I found it by accident," said Aunt Victoria. "I went on a ballooning vacation and, one misty morning, I discovered Monster Valley. I was so entranced by its beauty that I forgot to look where I was going."

"What happened?" I asked.

"I fell over a monster," said Aunt Victoria. "I had to leapfrog over its back to get away." Aunt Victoria sighed and shook her head. "It was very unfortunate, but I had to put my hands on its back to leapfrog, and I accidently pulled out some of its hair."

"Ouch," I said. "I bet it was annoyed."

"You could say that," said Aunt Victoria, nodding. "I suppose it had a right to be annoyed, since I'd trespassed on its territory and pulled out its hair."

"So why do you call it the Paintbrush Monster?" I asked.

"Because I made the monster's hair into a paintbrush to remind me of that adventure," said Aunt Victoria. She took out a paintbrush with purple hair at the end.

"Cool!" I said. "But I don't understand why Monster Valley isn't on the map."

"Because nobody knows it's there," said Aunt Victoria.

"You know it's there," I pointed out. "Why didn't you have it put on the map? Just think, you could have named it after yourself! The Victoria Juggins Monster Valley!"

"I couldn't do that!" Aunt Victoria sounded shocked. "If I told people where the valley was, everyone would be there in a flash, hunting the monster. My lips are sealed."

"Well, can you tell me what the monster looked like?" I begged.

Aunt Victoria laughed. "I can do better than that, Toby. I can paint you a picture!" She clapped her hands. "In fact, I can paint a monster set, one picture for every monster I've met! Oh, why didn't I think of that before?"

"I don't want to imagine," said my father in a gloomy voice. "Should I ask what it is you didn't think of before, Victoria?"

Aunt Victoria and I turned around to look at my father. He must have come up the stairs while we were talking.

"Hello, William!" Aunt Victoria beamed. "Toby's given me the most wonderful idea!"

"Oh dear," said my father. "Go and get your coat, Toby, but hurry back. I don't think I'm going to like this. I think I'm suffering from Victoria-itis."

I went to get my coat from Aunt Victoria's kitchen. When I came back to the studio, my father had his fingers in his ears and was refusing to listen.

"No!" cried my father. "Not monsters, Victoria! People will think you're crazy!"

"Crazy?" Aunt Victoria looked puzzled.

"Eccentric, then," said my father. "People will think you're very eccentric if you start painting pictures of monsters. And, if they think you're eccentric, they'll think I am eccentric, too. I am your brother, after all, and they'll think it runs in the blood."

"Nonsense!" said Aunt Victoria. "I might be eccentric, but anyone can see you are boringly sane."

My father began to protest again, but Aunt Victoria held up her hand. "Not another word, William! I'm going to do it, and that's that."

My father and I went home, leaving Aunt Victoria to work on her monster set.

"Toby," said my father solemnly as we walked home through the streets, "I am a broken man. Make sure you tell your Aunt Victoria that the next time you see her. And please give me one of those peppermints. I feel a case of monster-itis coming on."

"I'll remember," I said, handing over a peppermint. My father always acts like this whenever Aunt Victoria has an idea. Secretly, I think he's rather proud of her.

My father and I went back to Aunt Victoria's house the next day. We wanted to make sure she had remembered to eat.

Naturally, Aunt Victoria was upstairs in her studio. She was painting the first picture for her monster set. She had only got as far as the background, which was a misty valley. She was pleased to see us, especially when I went into the kitchen and made her a cheese-and-pickle sandwich.

"Can you paint me a pink dragon with hairy toenails?" I asked when I rejoined them in the studio.

"Don't be silly," said Aunt Victoria severely. "Pink dragons don't have hairy toenails. You must have them mixed up with the green ones. *Viridis hirsutus*, if you want the Latin name. *Viridis* means 'green' and *hirsutus* means 'hairy,' more or less."

"Dragons don't exist," said my father out of the corner of his mouth.

Aunt Victoria gave my father a scathing look and went on talking.

"I'm painting the Paintbrush Monster I met in Monster Valley," she said, pointing to her painting of a misty valley.

A week later, Aunt Victoria finished the Paintbrush Monster painting, and you should have seen it! (Maybe you *have* seen it, since it's really quite famous and is hanging in the National Treasure Gallery.)

"Aunt Victoria," I said solemnly, "this is the very best picture you've ever painted."

Usually, Aunt Victoria laughs when I say something like that, but, this time, she gave me a thoughtful look and smiled. "You know what, Toby? I think you might be right!"

Chapter Three

Mimi Maxwell
Asks for Proof

Once she started the monster set, there was no stopping Aunt Victoria. She painted and painted for weeks, until she had finished.

"These are glorious!" said my father when Aunt Victoria had finished the last one.

"I'm going to exhibit the set at the National Treasure Gallery," said Aunt Victoria.

The exhibition was a huge success. By the end of the opening night, every one of the monster paintings had a red "sold" sticker on its frame. There was one thing that pleased Aunt Victoria more than anything else though.

"The Gallery has bought one of the paintings as a permanent exhibit!" she told my father and me. "That's a great honor."

"Which one?" asked my father.

"I bet it's the Paintbrush Monster," I said. "That's the one I'd buy if I had a gallery."

Aunt Victoria clapped her hands. "That's right! That's the one they chose."

Even the newspapers began to take notice of Aunt Victoria's success. They printed a big photograph of Aunt Victoria and her paintings on the front page.

"Also, I've been asked to appear on a TV show," said Aunt Victoria.

"What show?" My father sounded nervous.

"It's *The Mimi Maxwell Show*, actually."

"*The Mimi Maxwell Show*! *The Mimi Maxwell Show*!" shrieked my father.

"Lots of people watch it," said Aunt Victoria defensively.

"Weirdos watch it," said my father. "It's the laughingstock of the airwaves!"

Aunt Victoria sighed. "I know, but it will give my paintings popular exposure. Besides, some people might call me a weirdo, too!"

My father muttered and grumbled, but he couldn't deny that. "Give me a peppermint, please, Toby," he said. "I need something to take my mind off my weird relation. I feel a case of weird-itis coming on."

Of course, my father and I made sure we were watching *The Mimi Maxwell Show* on the night of Aunt Victoria's appearance.

"She looks nervous," I said as Aunt Victoria settled in an armchair across from Mimi.

"So would I," said my father.

Mimi Maxwell was dressed in a red suit. She wore bright red lipstick and pointy shoes. She smiled straight at the camera.

"Good evening, viewers, and welcome to *The Mimi Maxwell Show*!"

"Look at those teeth!" said my father. "I bet she's a vampire in disguise."

"My first guest today is a monster expert," said Mimi Maxwell. "Let me introduce Victoria Juggins!"

Aunt Victoria gave a small smile.

"I understand you're a monster specialist, Victoria," said Mimi Maxwell.

Aunt Victoria shrugged. "I wouldn't say that, exactly, but I have met a few monsters in my travels."

"Oh, really? I suppose you're referring to the Egyptian Sphinx and other statues and monuments?"

"Oh no, I mean real monsters. The first one I met was the Loch Ness Monster," said Aunt Victoria. "It ate my camera!" She began to relax as she told the story. After that, she told the one about the yeti and the banana.

The studio audience laughed, and my father squirmed.

"She's making a fool of herself!" he said. "Mimi Maxwell is just encouraging her! Toby, please give me a peppermint. I feel a case of Mimi-Maxwell-itis coming on."

Mimi Maxwell leaned forward. "So, Victoria, are you actually claiming that these paintings – the monster set you have just exhibited – have been painted from real life?"

"No, of course not!" said Aunt Victoria.

Mimi looked puzzled. "But you have seen the living monsters? Or so you claim?"

"Yes, but I didn't paint them then…"

Mimi pounced. "So these paintings are completely imaginary? You haven't seen these monsters at all?"

"Of course I have," said Aunt Victoria.

My father groaned and banged his head with his fists.

Mimi Maxwell smiled slyly. "Maybe I should rephrase that question. You have no actual proof of meeting these creatures?"

"Oh yes!" said Aunt Victoria. She bent down and opened her purse, then brought out the paintbrush she had shown me.

"Here you are!" said Aunt Victoria. "This is made from the hair of the Paintbrush Monster of Monster Valley."

Mimi Maxwell took the paintbrush and held it up to the light. "Very impressive!" she said in a voice that meant just the opposite. "But surely a photograph would have been better proof than this!"

"I've just told you," said Aunt Victoria patiently, "the Loch Ness Monster ate my camera and I didn't get a new one. I took up painting after that."

"So you relied on memory to re-create these monsters you claim to have seen?"

"Ye-es," said Aunt Victoria.

"Hmm, quite a dilemma!" said Mimi Maxwell. She turned to face the camera.

"Since this so-called monster expert has no evidence of the adventures she *claims* to have had, apart from a paintbrush she *claims* to have made from the hair of a monster she *claims* to have seen..." Mimi paused to let the studio audience laugh, then continued, "it looks as if someone will need to find one of these monsters to prove it really exists outside Victoria Juggins's imagination."

Aunt Victoria squirmed in her seat.

"It might be best to start with the one monster for which there is possibly a shred of evidence, the so-called Paintbrush Monster of Monster Valley." Mimi Maxwell whipped out an atlas and a highlighter pen.

"Now, Victoria, if you'll show us exactly where this Monster Valley can be found, perhaps we may be able to begin."

"I'm not at liberty to do that," said Aunt Victoria, as Mimi Maxwell went on waving the highlighter pen and the atlas.

Mimi Maxwell must have made a signal because, suddenly, the camera zoomed in close to her face. She seemed to be peering out of the television, right at my father and me.

"It doesn't look good, does it, folks?" said Mimi Maxwell. "No proof, no photographs, and now the monster expert has suddenly lost the way to Monster Valley. Maybe there'll be a few red faces at the National Treasure Gallery? Hmmm?"

The camera switched to Aunt Victoria's face. She looked as if she might cry.

My father sighed. "That's done it," he said. "Are there any peppermints left? I'm sure I'm suffering from Victoria-itis."

Chapter Four

Sperrington Smithers Arrives

"The people from the gallery won't take any notice of a silly show like that, will they?" I asked my father, but he looked even more gloomy than usual.

"Other people *will* take notice, Toby, and there will be a lot of talk. The gallery will have to do something. It was all right while everyone thought the paintings were just imaginary. But, now that your aunt has claimed that monsters really exist, and hasn't been able to supply any proof, the gallery will feel embarrassed." My father looked dismal.

And, unfortunately, he was right. Over the next couple of weeks, there were several articles about it in the newspapers, and not one of them was kind to Aunt Victoria.

"I tried to explain to Mimi Maxwell why I won't tell the location of Monster Valley, but the station cut to a commercial break," said Aunt Victoria. "Now the gallery people have made me take back the Paintbrush Monster painting, and the people who bought the others in the set have returned theirs, too."

"Why don't they want them anymore?" I asked. "The paintings are just as good, whether you believe in monsters or not."

"Yes," said my father heavily as he read the newspapers, "but people hate to think they've been made to look like fools. Never mind, Victoria. The fuss will die down eventually."

"I suppose so," said Aunt Victoria. "I can't see why it should bother me. I'm used to being disbelieved, even by you, William."

My father looked embarrassed. "I don't disbelieve you exactly, Victoria," he said. "I just think your imagination runs away with you at times. Look, why don't you just tell people what they want to know?"

"I can't do that," said Aunt Victoria. "If people knew where to find Monster Valley, they'd hunt the Paintbrush Monster."

"*I* believe in your monster," I said.

"Thank you, Toby," said Aunt Victoria. "I think you're the only person who does!"

However, it turned out that there was somebody else who believed in Aunt Victoria's monster. He turned up at her house one day and said he wanted to buy every painting in the monster set.

"Okay," said Aunt Victoria. "And you are?"

"Mr. Sperrington Smithers is the name, monster fun is the game!" said the person on the doorstep. He shook Aunt Victoria's hand.

"This is my nephew, Toby," said Aunt Victoria politely.

"Hello, Mr. Smithers," I said.

Sperrington Smithers ignored me. Instead of shaking my hand, he whipped out a roll of money. "How much for Monster Valley, Ms. Juggins?"

"I beg your pardon?"

"How much for Monster Valley?" repeated Sperrington Smithers. "Come along, don't be coy. I'm a busy man."

"Why do you want to know?"

Sperrington Smithers smiled. "Well, you see, Ms. Juggins, I'm a property developer, and I'm interested in developing a Monster World Motel and Theme Park."

"You don't need Monster Valley for that," said Aunt Victoria. "There are plenty of other places."

"Ah, but how many of them have real monsters?" asked Sperrington Smithers. "Just name your price."

"I certainly will not!" huffed Aunt Victoria. "Monster Valley isn't mine to sell."

"I'm not asking you to sell the valley," said Sperrington Smithers. "I'm asking you to sell me the information about how to get there!"

"Well, I won't!" said Aunt Victoria.

Sperrington Smithers shrugged. "Oh well, I'll just buy the paintings then. I understand they've all been returned to you?"

"Yes, but..." stammered Aunt Victoria.

"I suppose it's all right if I pay you in cash?" Sperrington Smithers interrupted.

Aunt Victoria looked a bit startled, but she accepted. "I'll write you a receipt," she said.

As soon as I helped put the last painting in the car, Sperrington Smithers got in. He started the engine, rolled down the electric window, then looked out at Aunt Victoria.

"Now," he said, and he wasn't smiling anymore, "suppose we stop all this nonsense and you tell me exactly where to find this Monster Valley, Ms. Juggins!"

"No," said Aunt Victoria.

"You might as well," said Sperrington Smithers. "I'll find out eventually. It may take some time, but I *will* find out. Save us both a lot of trouble and tell me now!"

Aunt Victoria turned red, then pale. "I've changed my mind!" she said sharply. "I don't want to sell you my paintings! Give them back and take your money."

Sperrington Smithers laughed. "Too late," he said. "I've got them now, and at least one of them is worth its weight – in monsters."

He rolled up the window and drove off, leaving Aunt Victoria and me staring after him.

"What do you think he meant by that?" asked Aunt Victoria in a very small voice.

"He meant it was a really good painting," I said as I handed her a peppermint, but I didn't believe that, and neither did poor Aunt Victoria.

Chapter Five

Aunt Victoria
and I Depart

"I guess that's the end of that," said my father when Aunt Victoria told him about the ghastly Sperrington Smithers. "There's nothing he can do to find this Monster Valley of yours, Victoria. It has stayed hidden until now. Even Toby and I don't know where it is."

"I suppose so," said Aunt Victoria.

"I think Sperrington Smithers was just trying to upset you," said my father. "There's no way he can find that valley."

Unfortunately, my father was wrong. The three of us were watching television one night when Aunt Victoria gave a squeak of horror.

She spluttered, pointed at the television, and said, "Look! There's Sperrington Smithers on *The Mimi Maxwell Show*!"

Sure enough, there was Mimi Maxwell in her red suit and pointy shoes, and there, beside her, was Sperrington Smithers.

"Our regular viewers will remember the Victoria Juggins case we featured a few weeks ago," Mimi said. "Ms. Juggins is the artist who claims to have met real monsters, but a brief interview on this show was enough to point out the weakness of her story." Mimi smirked.

My father groaned. "Quick, I need a peppermint! I'm getting monster-itis again."

"However," continued Mimi, "I have here someone who claims to have searched out the mystery location. Let me introduce business entrepreneur Mr. Sperrington Smithers."

The studio audience applauded, and Aunt Victoria moaned.

"Sperrington," Mimi asked, "would you care to explain how you discovered the location Juggins refused to reveal?"

Sperrington Smithers chuckled. "Well, there wasn't much searching to be done, Mimi. You might say the lady told me herself!"

"So, you charmed it out of her," said Mimi.

"Not exactly," said Sperrington Smithers, chuckling again. "I bought this painting." He displayed Aunt Victoria's painting of the Paintbrush Monster and pointed to the plants in the foreground.

"It was simple," he crowed. "You see these flowers and leaves?"

I heard Aunt Victoria moan again.

"I hired a botanist to examine these plants. He told me that these very rare plants live only in one small part of one particular continent!" boasted Sperrington Smithers.

"Which continent is that?" asked Mimi.

Sperrington Smithers smiled. "That would be telling," he said. "Why should I spill the beans that I paid for?"

"You're not going to tell us where Monster Valley lies?" asked Mimi.

"You will know soon enough," said Sperrington Smithers. "I've taken steps to acquire the valley and, in six months, I'll open the Monster Valley Motel and Theme Park!"

"Six months?" Mimi Maxwell whistled. "How will you get it finished in time?"

"I believe in hands-on developing," said Sperrington Smithers. "I'll be there with the workers every step of the way."

"All this must have cost a great deal of money," said Mimi Maxwell.

Sperrington Smithers grinned and rubbed his hands. "The Monster Valley Motel and Theme Park is going to make me very rich. Monster rides, monster hunts, not to mention a monster-shaped swimming pool…"

"You have big ideas!" said Mimi.

"My dear," said Sperrington Smithers, "my ideas aren't just big, they're monstrous!"

My father turned off the television. Aunt Victoria was totally depressed.

"This is all my fault!" she wailed. "If only I'd been more careful. If only I wasn't such a good painter. If only I'd never been born."

"If only you'd stop wailing!" said my father. "It's done now, Victoria. I know you regret it, but there's nothing you can do."

"Oh, yes there is!" snapped Aunt Victoria. "I'm not beaten yet! I'm going to save the Paintbrush Monster from exploitation! I'm going to find it someplace else to live."

"Way to go, Aunt Victoria!" I whooped.

"Calm down, Victoria," said my father. "There must be a law protecting rare monsters from exploitation. These things should be dealt with through the proper channels."

"The proper channels take too long," said Aunt Victoria. "Toby, hand me the telephone."

"What are you doing?" asked my father.

"I'm going to spend the money Sperrington Smithers paid for the paintings," said Aunt Victoria. "I may not be able to prevent him from exploiting Monster Valley, but I *can* save the monster!"

Aunt Victoria punched in a telephone number. "Getaway Airways? I'd like to book two seats please, for Victoria and Toby Juggins."

Aunt Victoria was going to take me monster hunting with her! I thought that was the coolest thing ever.

My father didn't think so. "You can't take Toby! It's ridiculous. It's dangerous."

"It's educational," said Aunt Victoria. "And, besides, I need his help."

"I'll come instead," said my father.

That was really noble, because my father hates travel. He claims it gives him travel-itis.

Aunt Victoria shook her head. "I need a believer, William. I need Toby."

"All right, all right! But, Victoria, I'm relying on you to be sensible. Keep Toby out of trouble, and make sure you bring him back before school starts again."

Aunt Victoria promised, but I think she had her fingers crossed at the time.

While we waited for the day of our flight, I bought a supply of peppermints for myself and another bag to leave for my father, just in case he got lonely-itis while I was away. Meanwhile, Aunt Victoria sat down and designed a portable monster trap. As she said, it was no good expecting the monster to walk up and let her save it.

"It's a wild animal, Toby," she said. "If we had the time, we could tame it and win its trust. But, as it is, we must rescue it before Sperrington Smithers and his bulldozers and workers arrive."

We packed our bags and the monster trap, then my father drove us to the airport.

"I wish you'd do this through the proper channels," said my father. He hugged me, then he hugged Aunt Victoria.

It took a long time to get to Monster Valley. We flew in a big plane, then in a little plane, then in a tiny plane. After that, we flew in a hot-air balloon that Aunt Victoria had brought with her, all packed up in a crate.

"Why a balloon?" I asked Aunt Victoria after the tiny plane had flown away.

"Well, Toby, the commercial airlines don't have flights to Monster Valley," said Aunt Victoria. "And the fewer people who know where we're going, the better!"

"But who's going to fly us?" I asked.

"I am," said Aunt Victoria. "If you remember, I told you I was ballooning when I first found Monster Valley."

Aunt Victoria started up the burner, and the large, flabby balloon began to fill with air. Soon it was towering above us. It was a dull green color, so it would be camouflaged among the trees in the valley.

I gulped as I took my place in the basket. Going monster hunting with Aunt Victoria had seemed a good idea at home, but now I wasn't so sure!

Chapter Six

I See a Part of the Paintbrush Monster

Our balloon drifted north for a long time, first over towns, then, later, over strange, exotic forests. I stood in the basket, peering at the view through Aunt Victoria's binoculars.

Eventually, Aunt Victoria said, "Look, Toby, it's Monster Valley."

I looked down, and there, in the forest, I saw a grassy valley. The sides of the valley were rocky and sheer. They looked much too steep to climb. It looked very, very peaceful and still, like something out of a fairy tale.

"How is Sperrington Smithers going to build a motel here?" I asked. "And how are people going to get to it once it's built? Will they come by balloon, like us, or jump out of planes with parachutes?"

"Bulldozers will come and clear the forest," said Aunt Victoria. "Then they will build roads, bring in building materials, and probably construct a gondola to carry people in and out of the valley."

Aunt Victoria carefully landed the balloon. "We must hurry," she said. "There's not much time for exploring. We have to find the monster and trap it before Sperrington Smithers and the bulldozers come."

"How long do we have?" I asked as I climbed out of the basket.

"I don't know," said Aunt Victoria. "If the motel is to be opened in six months, the bulldozers could be here in a week or so. As it is, the builders will have to work around the clock. I don't want to be here when they arrive. Although Sperrington Smithers isn't evil, he's greedy and hard-hearted."

I was looking around, wondering how we were ever going to find the monster, when I heard a roaring sound in the distance. After that came a long drawn-out creak and a crash.

"The monster!" I gasped.

"No, Toby," said Aunt Victoria. "The Paintbrush Monster doesn't sound like that. I'm afraid it means that Sperrington Smithers has sent in the bulldozers already!"

"We'd better find the Paintbrush Monster right now," I said.

We searched among trees and behind rocks and, after a while, I wasn't so sure that I really did want to find the monster. What if it was ferocious? I could feel a case of my father's monster-itis coming on.

"Look!" said Aunt Victoria, taking my arm. "There it is!"

"What? Where?"

"There! It's asleep. Use your eyes!"

I peered through the bushes. Then I saw the Paintbrush Monster. That is, I saw part of it, just a long purple tail and one big foot with claws. The rest of the monster was hidden. I gulped and backed away. It looked so much bigger than it had in the painting. It also looked so much more real.

"I believe it's the only one of its kind," whispered Aunt Victoria. "It's certainly not like any of the other monsters I've met."

"There have to be others. You can't have just one of anything," I said.

Aunt Victoria shrugged. "That's usually the way it goes, but monsters are different. They're unique, quite unlike other animals. Sometimes there *is* only one of each kind. And there won't be even one Paintbrush Monster if Sperrington Smithers destroys its habitat."

"But they must come from somewhere," I insisted.

"Maybe they're mutations," said Aunt Victoria. "Something changes in an animal's DNA and it goes on from there. Say a snake lays twenty eggs. Nineteen of them hatch into baby snakes, but the twentieth egg hatches a newt instead. Or say an ordinary animal has four offspring. Three are normal and the fourth one is a Paintbrush Monster."

"That's weird," I said.

"Never mind that," said Aunt Victoria. "We have to catch that monster!"

I gulped again. I couldn't take my gaze off that tail and those claws.

"Hmmmm," I said. I swallowed – hard. Not that I was scared of the monster, exactly. Oh, of course I was! You would have been, too, if you'd been there!

Aunt Victoria certainly wasn't scared. She left me behind to make sure the monster didn't steal away while she went to get the monster trap from the balloon.

I bit my nails as I waited, but it wasn't long before I heard Aunt Victoria creeping back across the valley floor.

"Here it is," she said in a low voice, and she set the monster trap down in front of me.

All that was left to do was wait for the monster to wake up.

Chapter Seven

We Catch a Monster

"I do hope it won't sleep too long," said Aunt Victoria half an hour later, when the monster still gave no sign of moving out from behind the bush. "We have to get away from here before the bulldozers come."

"Can't we wake it up?" I asked, although I didn't really like the idea.

"Better not," said Aunt Victoria. "We don't want to frighten it."

Just then, the monster did wake up. First it stretched its tail and feet, then it sneezed, and then it slowly crawled out from behind the bush. Now I could see that it was a sort of mottled brownish purple color, like shadows in twilight. It had soft, leathery skin with scaly patches and tufts of purplish hair.

The tail we had seen already, as well as the fearsome claws. It also had a long nose, like the beak of a bird, and two gleaming tusks.

It yawned and peered at the monster trap.

"It's going to go in!" I whispered.

The monster sniffed the sausage Aunt Victoria had hung in the doorway of the trap as bait. Then it turned away with a bored look and wandered off.

"Oh, no!" said Aunt Victoria as the monster ambled across the valley. "It doesn't like that sausage. We'll have to try a different kind of bait."

We put some apples in the trap, but the monster wasn't interested in those either.

"I don't suppose it has ever seen apples before, or sausage," I said. "But, if the monster won't go into the trap, we'll just have to put the trap around the monster."

"Good idea! That's exactly what we'll do," said Aunt Victoria. "Climb up that tree over there, but be careful you don't fall."

While I clambered up the tree, Aunt Victoria closed the monster trap, removed the bottom, and tied a rope to the top.

"Catch!" called Aunt Victoria, and she tossed me the rope. I caught it and passed it over the branch. Then Aunt Victoria pulled on the rope, heaving the trap off the ground.

"Now, Toby," said Aunt Victoria calmly, "the next part is easy. When the monster runs under the tree, all you have to do is drop the trap neatly over its head."

"I can't!" I said.

"Of course you can," said Aunt Victoria. "You'll have no trouble at all."

Now, if Aunt Victoria says something can be done, I believe her. So there I sat, up in the tree, with the monster trap dangling on the end of a rope. I clung to the branch with my legs, longing for a peppermint.

"How are you going to get the monster to run under the tree?" I asked.

"Just like this," said Aunt Victoria.

I knew Aunt Victoria was very brave because of all her adventures, but I certainly didn't expect her to do what she did next! She jumped out of the shadows and waved her arms crazily at the Paintbrush Monster.

"Come and get me!" called Aunt Victoria in an annoying voice.

It certainly did annoy the Paintbrush Monster, for it roared indignantly and began to chase Aunt Victoria between the trees, all around the valley.

Suddenly, Aunt Victoria ran toward the tree where I was perched. "Now!" she yelled. "You can do it! Drop the trap now!"

I held my breath and dropped the trap right over the top of the Paintbrush Monster.

"We did it!" panted Aunt Victoria, jumping on top of the trap to hold it down.

"Great!" I cheered, but softly, because I didn't want to upset the monster.

I slithered down from the tree and helped Aunt Victoria slide the bottom of the trap in.

After a long while, I sat down and opened my bag of peppermints. I had only just put one in my mouth when the Paintbrush Monster sniffed the air. Its tail lashed back and forth and it started to whine.

"What's wrong with it?" I asked. "It isn't hurt, is it?"

The Paintbrush Monster sniffed again. Its purple nostrils quivered.

"I think it wants a peppermint," said Aunt Victoria. "It reminds me of your father. It probably thinks it has trap-itis."

Do you know what? Aunt Victoria was right. The monster *did* want a peppermint!

Very carefully, I threaded one of my peppermints on a flat stick and held it out to the Paintbrush Monster. Soon, the monster was crunching the peppermint down, licking its lips, and begging for more.

"Maybe just two wouldn't hurt it," said Aunt Victoria.

The monster ate the second peppermint, then went to sleep.

"Now, let's get out of here and take this monster somewhere safe before it wakes up and gets all upset again!" said Aunt Victoria.

It was hard work, but we managed to drag the monster trap, with the sleeping monster inside, back to the balloon. Then, with one final effort, we lifted the trap into the basket.

Aunt Victoria started the burner and we waited for the balloon to fill with hot air.

"I wish this balloon would hurry up and fill," said Aunt Victoria with a sigh. "Those bulldozers sound awfully close."

I listened, and Aunt Victoria was right. They sounded much closer than before.

"Hurry up, balloon!" muttered Aunt Victoria, but the balloon was still only about half-full when the first bulldozer reached the rim of Monster Valley and rocked forward to begin the downward trip.

"Oh, no!" cried Aunt Victoria. "Look who's driving that bulldozer, Toby!"

I picked up her binoculars from the bottom of the basket and peered up at the bulldozer.

"That's Mr. Smithers!" I exclaimed. "I don't believe it! He's going to catch us!"

The balloon was filling fast, but not fast enough. Sperrington Smithers jumped out of his bulldozer and scrambled desperately toward us, waving his arms and rushing down the hill like a furious whirlwind.

"Not so fast, Victoria Juggins!" he yelled. "That's my monster you've got in there!"

Chapter Eight

The Paintbrush Monster Hitches a Ride

Sperrington Smithers climbed into the balloon basket and turned off the burner. He stared at the Paintbrush Monster, which was still asleep in the trap.

"What a lazy looking thing!" he said. "Have you drugged it? Are you sure it's alive?"

"Of course it's alive!" hissed Aunt Victoria. "And of course I haven't drugged it!"

"Just as well for you!" snorted Smithers. "If you'd killed my monster, I would have sued you! In fact, I still might sue you for trying to steal it. Unless, of course, you immediately release it into my custody."

There was nothing we could do. We had to watch while Sperrington Smithers opened the monster trap.

"Out, you!" he yelled, and he poked the monster with a stick. "Get yourself out into Monster Valley where you belong!"

The Paintbrush Monster had been fast asleep in the trap, but it woke up with a start when Sperrington Smithers prodded it. Its purple eyes opened wide and it shot out of the trap with a snarl and a roar. Next, it reared up on its hind legs and waved its claws like daggers. It swished its tail and flashed its tusks around in an arc that came very close to Sperrington Smithers's head.

"Aaaiieee!" wailed Sperrington Smithers. He leaped out of the basket and ran for his life up the steep side of Monster Valley. The Paintbrush Monster ran after him. Sperrington Smithers scrambled and slithered and yelped as he fled to his bulldozer, with the monster chasing him.

I laughed and laughed. I was sure the Paintbrush Monster wasn't really going to hurt Sperrington Smithers. If it had meant to eat him, it could have caught him easily.

In fact, I'd almost decided the Paintbrush Monster wasn't really fierce at all. It just liked playing chasing games!

"Look at him run! It serves him right," I said, but Aunt Victoria was worried.

"We haven't solved anything, Toby," she said. "We've probably made things even worse than they were already."

"But Sperrington Smithers won't dare hurt the monster now," I said. "He's too scared of it!"

Aunt Victoria sighed. "Some people can't bear to be made to look like a fool, Toby," she said, "and the Paintbrush Monster has just made Sperrington Smithers look very foolish indeed. I'm afraid it will make him even more determined to exploit the monster in any way he can."

"Oh," I said. "So what can we do now?"

Aunt Victoria sighed as she turned on the burner. "I think we should just go home, Toby. William is right. There must be a law to keep Sperrington Smithers from exploiting a very rare monster. We really should have tried to do things through the proper channels. If we attempt to catch the monster again, Sperrington Smithers will probably sue us."

The balloon finished filling and we took off. We began to rise up over the rim of the misty bowl, past a clump of tall trees. I turned for a last glimpse of Monster Valley and, just at that moment, there came a loud roar from the tallest tree.

The balloon basket suddenly swayed and bounced and I nearly fell out.

"Help!" I yelled, but it was only the Paintbrush Monster. It had jumped out of the tree and was scrambling over the edge of the basket behind me.

"You clever monster!" cried Aunt Victoria as soon as she managed to steady the balloon. "You understand exactly what we're trying to do!"

"Won't Sperrington Smithers sue us?" I asked. "We're taking his monster."

Aunt Victoria considered. "It did come with us of its own accord," she said. "And I'm afraid Mr. Smithers certainly wasn't acting as if he liked it very much."

I squatted down and leaned against the Paintbrush Monster. It was nice and warm and it didn't seem to mind, especially when I offered it a peppermint.

We brought the balloon down in the middle of a swamp.

"Perfect!" said Aunt Victoria as we landed. "Not even Sperrington Smithers would try to build a motel and theme park on ground like this. The foundations would sink."

"Will the monster like it here?" I asked as I looked around. It seemed a bit dank to me. It was nothing like the wonderful, magical valley where the monster had lived before.

"I hope it will like it here," said Aunt Victoria. "It's got to be better than being hunted or displayed as a zoo exhibit, wouldn't you agree, Toby?"

I nodded. Maybe the place didn't look very wonderful to me, but, then again, it certainly looked better than any of Mr. Smithers's plans.

Aunt Victoria coaxed the Paintbrush Monster out of the basket with two more peppermints. It galloped off into the forest, spattering bits of moss and turf as it went.

"There!" said Aunt Victoria. "Now it will be safe."

It was getting dark, and it seemed too late to take off in the balloon again, so Aunt Victoria and I camped in the swampy forest. I'm afraid we didn't get much sleep, because an eerie howling noise began as soon as the stars came out.

"What on earth is that?" I gasped.

"Monstersong," said Aunt Victoria calmly. "Most monsters sing at night, Toby. There's nothing to worry about."

In the morning, we fired up the burner again. The balloon filled and lifted and the basket began to rock, then to drag across the swampy floor. Suddenly, the Paintbrush Monster came rushing out of the forest with a howl, trying to hitch another ride.

"Help!" I yelled as the Paintbrush Monster took a flying leap and landed in the basket. The balloon swayed violently, and the Paintbrush Monster started licking Aunt Victoria's feet.

Aunt Victoria moved her feet out of the way. "This is very flattering, Painty," she said.

"But you're supposed to be living in the forest!" She gave the Paintbrush Monster a push, but it sat down and dug in its claws. It simply refused to go.

"Maybe it doesn't like this place," I said. "We could find somewhere nicer."

"I suppose so," said Aunt Victoria, and up we went again, monster and all.

I expect you can guess what happened in the end. The monster just didn't want us to leave it behind. Not in Monster Valley, not in the swampy forest. Not anywhere. We tried lots of places, but, in the end, we ran out of time and Aunt Victoria had to take it home.

"I don't think this is a good idea, Toby," she said. She sounded worried. "I do not approve of removing monsters from their natural habitats."

"But, if you don't take it, it's just going to run after the balloon," I said, and Aunt Victoria had to agree.

We packed away the balloon, then caught the tiny plane, and, later on, the two bigger ones. The Paintbrush Monster had to spend the whole trip traveling in the back with the luggage because none of the pilots would let it sit in the seat beside Aunt Victoria.

My father was waiting for us at the Getaway Airways counter.

"Toby!" he exclaimed, and gave me a hug. Then he saw the Paintbrush Monster peering out of the monster trap. "Mercy! Mercy!" yelled my father. "Victoria, this is too much. You've brought a monster home! You can't keep a monster as a pet. You must know that! The mayor will never allow it!"

"Of course I know that, William," said Aunt Victoria crossly. "Painty will just stay with me until I can think of something better. In the meantime, I can paint more pictures and keep Painty safe from exploitation."

Chapter Nine

Aunt Victoria Sets Up a Fund

"You should sell a lot more monster pictures," I said. "They'll make you lots of money. You don't have to paint real monsters. You could do imaginary ones, like dragons and mermaids and griffins and things."

"But, Toby, they're not imagin..." began Aunt Victoria.

"Enough!" roared my father. "I have heard absolutely enough on this subject! Put that crate in the backseat, Victoria. I might be forced to believe in monsters, but that doesn't mean I want one sitting beside me. And give me a peppermint, Toby. I'm about to suffer from monster-itis."

We all got into the car and my father started to drive us home.

"What good would money do me now?" asked Aunt Victoria. "It wouldn't help me get Painty settled."

"Yes, it would," I argued. "With lots of money you could buy yourself a big section of forest and turn it into a monster reserve. No one would ever be able to knock it down or hunt monsters there if it belonged to you. You could build a house for yourself there, and the Paintbrush Monster could live in the reserve and visit you whenever it wanted. And you could rescue other monsters if their habitats were destroyed. Wouldn't that be a good thing to do?"

My father sighed. "For goodness' sake, Toby, don't encourage her!" Then he glanced in his rearview mirror. "Victoria, you are supposed to be a positive role model!"

I could see that my father definitely had a case of Victoria-itis coming on.

But, as my father turned our car onto Aunt Victoria's street, Aunt Victoria reached over the back of the seat and gave me a hug.

"You are brilliant, Toby!" she shrieked in my ear. "Absolutely brilliant!"

She jumped out of the car as soon as it stopped and danced with me around her yard. The Paintbrush Monster howled and yowled and roared until my father yelled at it to stop. After that, Aunt Victoria calmed down.

"Out you go, Painty," she said, opening the door of the monster trap and giving the Paintbrush Monster a scratch under its chin. "You'll have to live in my backyard until I get more pictures painted."

The Paintbrush Monster squirmed out of its trap and promptly climbed to the top of one of Aunt Victoria's garden sculptures. It made a sort of purring noise, closed its eyes, and fell asleep.

Aunt Victoria sighed. "If only I could have bought Monster Valley! That would have been the perfect place, Toby, but it's too late now. Sperrington Smithers owns it and he'll never sell it to me. Never mind, I can use the rest of the money he paid me for the monster set paintings to help buy a monster reserve."

My father and I went home soon after that.

"I hope your Aunt Victoria knows what she's doing," said my father. "She seems to have taken on a very big project, Toby."

"She can do it," I said. "Aunt Victoria is very smart."

"Oh, she's smart all right," said my father. "But that doesn't mean she's practical."

"What do you mean?" I reminded my father about all the things Aunt Victoria had done. "She can fly a balloon and tame a monster and she has all sorts of adventures. Aunt Victoria is a very special sort of person."

My father sighed. "She certainly is very special, Toby. She's one of the most interesting people I know. Unfortunately, she doesn't make life very easy for herself. I mean, really, meeting monsters?"

"But she *did* meet monsters," I pointed out. "You've seen the proof. Admit it, Dad. Once you'd seen the Paintbrush Monster, you had to admit that monsters are real."

"I did admit that all right," said my father. "I just wish your Aunt Victoria had pretended the monsters in the monster set paintings were only something she'd imagined. Then none of this trouble would have happened."

"You mean you wanted her to lie to people," I said bitterly.

"No!" My father was sounding exasperated by now. "I don't want her to lie. I just want her to let people believe what they believe already. I want her to let people believe the sensible thing. After all, you've seen lots of pictures of alien spacecraft, haven't you?"

I nodded. "I've got some posters of them."

"Right!" said my father. "You've got posters, but you don't stop to ask yourself if the people who painted them have really seen any UFOs, do you? You just presume they haven't, and that they made them up. You believe they're just imaginary paintings."

He had a point, I suppose.

Now that the Paintbrush Monster was living in Aunt Victoria's backyard, there was no way anyone could believe it didn't exist. In fact, Mimi Maxwell came around to visit Aunt Victoria and tried to get her to come back on the show with Painty.

Aunt Victoria told her to go away.

Mimi wasn't the only person to take an interest in the Paintbrush Monster, though.

Aunt Victoria's neighbors were also very interested in what went on in her backyard. Unfortunately, they weren't very pleased.

"That thing is dangerous," they said, pointing at Painty's tusks and claws.

Aunt Victoria showed them all how friendly Painty was. She let the neighbors feed him peppermints.

"That thing is noisy," they said.

They had a point there. Painty was fine during the day, but at night he liked to sit on Aunt Victoria's doorstep and howl his monstersong loudly.

"It's creepy," said the neighbors. "We don't like it. It keeps the children awake."

Aunt Victoria put Painty in the spare bedroom every night. That way, his songs were muffled. The windows quivered and rang like a tuning fork, but at least the neighbors could get some sleep.

They still complained about other things, though. "There are too many sightseers around here," they said. "We can hardly get out our own front doors because of all the visitors! There's nowhere to park our cars because the tour buses all come here so people can see the monster."

They had a point there as well. Visitors came from all over to take a look at the Paintbrush Monster. Aunt Victoria put out a collection box, hoping it would make them go away, but instead they dropped money in it. Soon, donations were coming through the mail as well.

Then, one day, the mayor came to visit Aunt Victoria.

"Hello," I said. I was helping out that day washing windows. "Would you like a cup of coffee, Mr. Broggen?"

The mayor shook his head. "No, Toby, I need to speak to your aunt."

I called for Aunt Victoria and she came down nervously from the studio. "Hello, Mr. Broggen. How can I help you?"

The mayor is a nice man, but he didn't look very happy. He cleared his throat.

"Look, Ms. Juggins, I hate to say this, but there have been a number of complaints about your monster," he said.

"I know," sighed Aunt Victoria. "But what can I do about it?"

"You can listen to reason," said the mayor. "You really shouldn't be collecting money the way you are. You're not a registered charity."

"I never said I was!" retorted Aunt Victoria. "Anyway, the money isn't for me, it's to save the monsters!"

"I'm sure it is," said the mayor, looking nervously at Painty. "And it's the monster that's the trouble. You'll have to get rid of it, Ms. Juggins. I don't mean shoot it or anything. I mean you'll have to find it somewhere else to live."

"That's what I'm trying to do," said Aunt Victoria. She told the mayor about the way we had tried to find a new home for the Paintbrush Monster, and how she was trying to earn enough money so she could buy some land and turn it into a monster reserve.

"I can see your problem," said the mayor, "but I'm afraid you'll have to find somewhere else for it to live right away. You simply can't keep that monster here any longer. It's against the zoning laws."

After the mayor had gone, Aunt Victoria sat down and wrung her hands.

"I don't know what to do, Toby," she said. "I have enough money to buy some land, but I haven't picked a place yet. It may take months!"

I really didn't have any ideas, so I offered to make Aunt Victoria a cheese-and-pickle sandwich.

She was just taking her first bite when my father arrived with some important news.

"It concerns you, Victoria," said my father. "It's about Sperrington Smithers."

"What about him?" asked Aunt Victoria.

"He's in trouble with the law," said my father. "It seems that in his rush to develop Monster Valley, he failed to apply for the correct development permits from the proper authorities. Now he faces a substantial fine."

"So?" said Aunt Victoria. "How does that affect me?"

"He has been forbidden to proceed with the development," said my father, "and it appears that he is now having big financial problems. So big, in fact, that he needs to sell Monster Valley as soon as he can."

My father smiled at Aunt Victoria. "Now, I'm sure you'll want to put in a bid, Victoria, but please, this time, go through the proper channels!"

Chapter Ten

Aunt Victoria Moves to a New Location

Well, all that happened three years ago, but there are just a few things left to relate.

You know, of course, that Aunt Victoria bought Monster Valley. She didn't have enough money right away, but the mayor and my father bought shares in the project and so did some people from the museum and a few other interested parties. Aunt Victoria sold her house and used the money to build a studio, which she calls the Victoria Juggins Gallery and Monster Reserve. She lives there most of the time, although she still visits me and my father from time to time.

How can you get to Monster Valley? Well, Sperrington Smithers's half-built road is growing over now, and anyone who wants to visit Aunt Victoria's studio has to fly in by balloon with someone else who knows the way.

Of course, you might think that makes things difficult for people who want to see the monsters and Aunt Victoria's paintings, but Aunt Victoria has solved that problem very neatly. She bought some computer equipment and a satellite Internet connection, then she set up Monstercam and Gallerycam. These are Internet sites that show what's happening in Monster Valley twenty-four hours a day!

Now, let's see... Oh yes! You probably think I made a mistake in Chapter One, when I said the Paintbrush Monster painting is in the National Treasure Gallery. It's true that the gallery manager did refuse to buy the painting, but, after Aunt Victoria set up Monstercam, the manager had a sudden change of heart.

He bought the whole monster set from Sperrington Smithers. Then he came to meet Painty and apologize to Aunt Victoria. He got so excited about Painty he even bought some stock in the monster reserve!

Painty is very happy, of course, and so are two other monsters that Aunt Victoria has managed to rescue.

I often spend my vacations in Monster Valley and, because I'm good with computers, Aunt Victoria has put me in charge of her latest on-line project. We call it Monster SOS and it's a web site devoted to information about monsters who might need rescuing. And that's all, except for this – if you have any news about monsters in distress, you can contact us at: *www.monstercam.edu/auntvictoria.*

From the Author

 Take one hero, a boy with common sense. Add a purple monster, a toothy talk-show journalist, a property developer, a sweet-natured artistic aunt, a hot-air balloon, and a rather boringly sane dad. Mix in a paintbrush, some peppermints, and a hidden valley, and what do you get? The story *Aunt Victoria's Monster*!

Some people love inventing recipes for cake. I love inventing recipes for stories. One day, I decided to invent a story that is one part family story, two parts adventure, one part animal story, and one part comedy. Here is the result.

Sally Odgers

From the Illustrator

 I envy Aunt Victoria having a Paintbrush Monster in her backyard. The nearest I've come to that is having a hairy guinea pig named Porky.

Like Aunt Victoria, I've traveled to many exotic places. In Nepal, I rode an elephant, but I didn't see a yeti. I've traveled to Scotland, but, alas, I didn't see the Loch Ness Monster. And, in India, I bought three fine paintbrushes made from pigs' eyelashes, which I've used on some of the illustrations in this book.

For my next adventure, I would like to stay on a ranch and ride Appaloosa horses like a real cowgirl. When I return home, I'll have to remember to bring some peppermints – not to feed to a Paintbrush Monster, but to treat Porky. He loves them, too!

Helen Bacon

Discussion Starters

1. Aunt Victoria isn't impressed by things that "everyone knows." Can you think of other examples of things that everyone knows, or used to know, that have been proved untrue, or are hotly debated?

2. Sperrington Smithers tries to exploit the rare Paintbrush Monster. Do you know of any other rare or endangered animals? How do you think such animals should be protected? Is it always best to go through "proper channels"?

3. The National Treasure Gallery makes Aunt Victoria take her Paintbrush Monster painting back after she says on television that she thinks monsters are real. Do you think that's fair? Does it matter whether the subject of a painting is real or imaginary?